COWBOYS' HOLIDAY AGE GAP

Fertile First Time Anthology

Leandra Camilli

ISBN: 9798797078401
Imprint: Independently published

1st edition

Cover design by: Leandra Camilli

CONTENTS

COWBOYS' LUCKY AGE GAP

Fertile First Time Thanksgiving Story

CHAPTER 1

Perhaps everything would be so much easier if that hunk of a man wasn't seated across from me. We were in the dining room, and I wasn't alone.

His colleague was also with us, picking up a glass of wine and taking a sip from it. His eyes were locked with mine and it was like he was trying to read my mind.

I wasn't trying to read his mind, but I was ogling him without making it obvious I was doing that. I had no idea if he was picking that up, but he smiled and I could see the beautifulness of his super white teeth.

I was just checking him out, wishing I could be in his arms. They looked so strong, confident, veins popping out where I could more easily see them, hair in all the right places, and his skin tanned by the light of the sun. I'd been fantasizing about him since coming here.

And it wasn't just Walter's arms that made my pussy wet, but also his face. And more specifically, his lips.

I wouldn't say that they were big, but they look just right and I knew that if I were kissing them now, I'd be tasting how sweet they were.

His face was chiseled and looked perfect. He groomed his full, thick beard every day, and it looked sharp without making him look gay.

It gave him that extra spice of manliness I always craved in a man. Looking down slightly, I also loved how his beard transitioned to his neck. I could just imagine myself lying in his bed with him and cradling my head in the crook of his neck. I was pretty sure he would love it if I did that.

But something was impeding me from doing that, and it was the fact that I was a virgin. I didn't know much about these two guys, but I knew that they craved women that had a lot more experience.

I didn't want to disappoint them or myself.

His blond hair seemed to draw my attention to him, and I couldn't control that I was ogling it too. It was short, a bit bigger at the top, and even shorter at the sides. I had no idea if he got his hair cut often, but it was always sharp. This wasn't the first time I was checking him out, after all.

His eyes were icy blue and I suddenly found myself entranced by them. His eyes showed me that behind his tough persona, he was a free-spirited and extroverted man. I didn't need that to tell me that was what he was like, but it was great having that confirmation again.

Seated beside him was his colleague. He was forking a piece of meat on his plate, and I noticed the veins popping out on his forearms. His skin was also white, but just as tanned.

He didn't have a full beard like Walter, but his stubble actually made him look sexier. I could just imagine what it would be like to be grazing my hands over his chin and jawline, feeling the roughness of his skin.

His lips were a little bigger than his friend's and the texture of his skin showed me that he was about the age of his colleague.

He was also looking at me with just one intention in his mind. Even though he wasn't going to say this to me now, I knew that he fantasized about me. He wanted to tell me that, but couldn't bring himself to do it.

Meanwhile, I was trying to survive this overly erotic, tense, and uncomfortable dinner. My nipples were hard and my pussy was wetter than it had ever been. I had no idea what I thought I was doing when I decided to come work here this summer.

We hadn't even said anything besides some very unimportant lines when we sat down.

It wasn't that they didn't like me or anything of the sort, but that two men and a woman seated at a table usually preceded them fucking. The fact that they had invited me over for dinner showed me how much they craved me.

Otis wore a somewhat loose checkered shirt that didn't fully occlude his muscles from my curious eyes.

I could see the lines of his pectorals, the subtle fur on his chest, and a line of sweat traveling down the region just under his neck. The skin there was slightly red too, telling me that he worked outside often and didn't mind the heat of the sun.

His eyes were jade green and just like his friend's, it was as if he was looking into my soul, I noticed as he bit into a piece of steak.

He was so big and tall that he made the chair he was sitting on look smaller than it was. Every time he moved, it made a creaking noise, as if it was complaining he was too heavy.

I was aware that the chairs in his farmhouse weren't new anymore, but that intermittent creaking noise still spoke volumes about his weight. It wasn't that he had a layer of fat in his body he should burn, but that his muscles were thick and dense.

There was one time I accidentally bumped against him, and it felt like I'd collided not against a human being, but a mountain.

My feet had slipped and I thought I was going to fall over on the ground, but he had quickly curved his arm around me and held me close to him.

It was then that I had really felt just how strong he was. My nipples had gone so hard that moment I was never going to forget it. Even now, thinking about it, I felt like I was going to explode if I didn't have sex with him.

I picked up a handkerchief off the table and wiped it over my mouth.

"I'm sorry, but I need to go to the bathroom," I said, and I was relieved that none of them objected.

I couldn't be in the same room with them anymore without feeling like my ovaries were going to explode.

CHAPTER 2

It looked like I'd made a mistake, but now I was in the bathroom everything was calm in here. I finally had some privacy, I thought after splashing some water on my face.

I needed to cool down after spending not even 20 minutes in the dining room. It was almost like it was a furnace.

I picked up a towel and dried my face with it, tossing it into the hamper when I didn't need it anymore. I opened the door and considered going back into the dining room. But then, the thought that if I did that I'd be making a huge mistake, popped up in my mind.

Going back to the dining room would not change anything. If anything, I would be falling into the same pattern as before. Looking at them for more than a second would keep making my pussy wetter.

It was with that thought in mind that I walked to the left, opened the door, and then went outside the farmhouse. My eyes soon spotted the barn on the other side, close to the fence.

There were many places on the farm where I liked to hang out at, but it was near the barn where I felt most comfortable.

I padded over there and leaned on the wall of the barn, putting my hands in my pockets. I didn't smoke, but now was the perfect moment for that.

I closed my eyes and listened to the sounds of nature around me. They were beautiful, especially the hooting of an owl in the distance.

My body twitched when I heard a strange noise coming from

within the barn. I whirled around, squinting my eyes as I tried to block out all other noises.

Doing that was difficult, but I was managing to. We didn't have any animals in the barn. That was why I was finding that noise weird. I'd been on their farm the whole day. I'd have known if they'd put cows in there.

It was true that they never let me enter the barn, saying something along the lines of 'it's not ready yet, and it's pretty dirty and nasty.'

I hadn't even bothered spying into the structure to find out if they were lying. When it came down to it, I didn't want to lose this job.

I took a deep breath, noticing a crack in the wall of the barn. If I could look through it, then I'd find out what was going on here. Perhaps I was imagining things. Either way, I wanted to find out if I was going crazy or not.

I put my hands on the sides of the hole to block out the moonlight, lowered my head, and peered inside the barn. Everything inside it was dark for a moment until I felt my eyes adjusting.

And when I could see the lines of what appeared to be a woman's ass pointed at me, I gasped. It had to have been just me imagining things that actually weren't there, right?

I moved my head away from the wall, shook it, and then peered into the barn again. I blinked until my eyes were getting adjusted to the darkness again.

The ass that was inside that pen was still there, and now it was shaking. It was like I wasn't dreaming this, and that there was indeed a woman inside the barn.

"What the actual fuck is going on-" I was saying when I felt a hand on my shoulder.

I whirled around, finding a very familiar face in front of me. That chiseled, perfect jawline, his jade-green eyes, and his pink-ish lips - I'd have known it was Otis even if he was wearing a disguise. But he wasn't. He was probably worried why I didn't show up back for dinner.

"What are you doing here?" He asked, making me suddenly

forget about the noise in the barn.

"I just wanted to get some fresh air," I responded and then suddenly remembered why I was feeling weird. "I think I just heard a noise in the barn."

"It's probably nothing," he said, waving his hand. "You're imagining things."

I pressed my hand to the wall of the barn and suddenly felt it going the other way. I was trying to support my weight, but now it was falling over into the structure! Otis jumped and grabbed me, but it was too late.

A part of the wall of the barn had fallen and left a huge hole. And through the hole, I finally could see what was in the structure.

Spotting women in pens, naked, with boobs bigger than I'd ever seen in my life, I knew that I was discovering something huge. Even Otis' eyes were looking conflicted. He never thought I was going to find out about this.

"What is this?" I asked, feeling like I was anywhere but on a typical farm. A group of women, naked like when they were born, were inside the pens, mooing as their eyes darted to us.

I could also see that they had been branded, and collars with small bells were hanging from their necks. Every time they moved, they jingled as milk dripped from their nipples.

I pushed myself out of his arms, looking into his eyes with a benign and surprised expression.

He put his hands on his waist and sighed. "Alright, guess that now you should know what's going on here."

CHAPTER 3

Each word that he said made me feel like I was in a movie. But then, he told me that I could be a part of it, too. Otis said that I could be like all the other hucows.

Even bigger than them, with curves wider than I ever thought possible and lips so full I'd think something was wrong with my genes when I was born.

It was one of the biggest choices of my life, but I didn't shy away from it. And he said that it could only be done in a certain way. I was in his bedroom, and my heart was in my throat.

He asked me not to be too surprised when he lowered his pants. He said that what I was going to see was going to leave me flabbergasted.

Otis opened the door of the room, his jade-green eyes shining in the darkness. Moonlight was coming through the window on my right, highlighting his perfect muscles and skin. My mouth was already watering even though we hadn't done anything special yet.

I was just surprised that I was finally going to have my first time with a man. I had no idea how he was going to react, only that he knew I was a virgin. He didn't tell me that, of course. It was clear he did in the way he was staring at me.

I gulped when he closed the door and started to lower his pants. When they were on his knees, my eyes went wide when I saw the size of his bulge.

It was bigger than I thought, and I could only wonder if he was even human. No man that I knew, not even in porn movies, was that big.

And it wasn't just that too, but also the thickness of his thighs and how hairy they were. I was a couple of feet away from him and I really wanted to be feeling his thighs with my hands. I wanted to worship him and I knew he was thinking the same thing.

Otis snuck his fingers under his boxers and lowered them, flashing a smile on his face. When his cock came out, it was bouncing up and down. He was uncut and something was telling me that his colleague was the same.

The skin looked taught, almost like it couldn't be stretched any further. Veins covered the whole surface of it, ending where his balls were. I looked slightly down and noticed how low they hung. I wanted to play with them using my fingers, and I knew that soon I was going to get the chance.

"This is it. If you want to end this and pretend that it didn't happen, this is your last chance," he murmured, looking straight into my eyes. Other than his perfect muscles and soft skin, the only thing I could see was his jade green eyes glaring at me.

I didn't say anything. I was inexperienced and shy.

Otis took a step toward me, making it so I could feel the heat of his body and his smell. It was a peculiar, manly smell that was very much like him.

Strong, showing off his independence, that he wasn't afraid of anything, and that he thought I was going to be just one more addition to his hucow team. After working here for so many weeks and suffering in the heat of the sun, I wanted something different.

He grabbed his cock and guided it to my mouth. I had no choice but to open it, and even then I felt that it wasn't enough. I felt like it was going to rip the flesh and the skin, making me feel more pain than I ever felt in my life.

And even though he was seeing how wide my eyes were going, he kept on pushing his hips forward and sliding his dick until he was balls-deep inside of me.

I was utterly dominated and subjugated to his desires, and I needed to swallow his come. That was the only way to become what I'd seen in the barn. I wanted to become a hucow like all of them.

Otis placed his hand on the back of my head and started to roll his hips. He was caring and forgiving at the beginning, mentioning nothing about the fact that I couldn't use my tongue to please him the way I wanted to.

I was giving a blowjob and, at the same time, I wasn't. He was incredibly thick and I could feel the heat of his shaft emanating from it, and it was everything I thought it was going to be.

The darkness in the room was actually working in my favor. It was making it so I could focus only on his cock ramming in and out of my mouth, striking the back of my throat over and over.

He was so thick that the friction was actually making this hotter than it would otherwise be. I could slightly taste his pre-come, and the way his balls were hitting against my chin was driving me so wild I was fingering myself even though I shouldn't.

His fingers dug deeper into the back of my head when his thighs tensed up all of a sudden. Locking my head where it was, Otis didn't hold back as he erupted inside my mouth. Jet after jet of his delicious milk flowed down my throat, gracing my stomach with its presence.

It was warm, salty, and I was loving everything it was making me feel. I never thought that it was possible to climax without more stimulation, but he was proving me otherwise.

He was filling me full with his come and wasn't even ashamed. In fact, looking up, I could see that what he was doing was making him feel proud of himself.

Moments later, he pulled out and slid his hand over my chin. It was his way of telling me that from now on I was going to be forever his and that nothing was going to change.

And now, it was going to be time for my first milking.

CHAPTER 4

Everything happened in so little time I was a very different person now. Walter opened the door of the farmhouse and I crawled out of it. I had a collar with a bell hanging from my neck, and it jingled every time I moved.

Now that my body was much bigger than it was before, it was difficult to move around only on my legs. I had to crawl around and even though some people thought it was a nuisance, I thought differently.

I could move while showing these two hunks what they were losing by not fucking me right at this moment.

A delicious, tight, and still virgin pussy for their thick cocks.

Otis was standing by the door of the barn, a victorious smile on his face. He was naked and I could see all the lines that defined his body, and I was only wondering when he was going to let me have a piece of him.

My boobs were so heavy that they were dragging over the ground as I made my way to that hunk.

My eyes were entirely focused on him and the massive dick hanging from between his legs. I wanted nothing more than to be rubbing my lips around it and taking all of it inside my mouth. I was sure he'd be pleased.

I put a hand on the grass by the house when I heard a slap and felt something hitting me hard on my ass.

I turned my head around slightly and smiled when I realized that it was Walter who had done that. He was naughty and would never hide that about him.

And seeing that he was going to get no reaction from me, he smiled as he grabbed his cock and stroked it gently.

He was teasing me and he knew he was doing that.

It took me more time than I thought it was going to, but I eventually reached the barn and then crawled into it.

All the other hucows mooed as they realized that I was coming in here for my first milking.

A machine was by one of the walls of the barn. It was big and a little intimidating, but nothing that was going to shy me away from doing this.

Walter pressed a button on it and it lowered. I crawled onto it and he pressed the same button again. He was stroking his cock gently as he watched me.

The machine stopped and then he attached two pumps to my udders, which were positioned just under the surface where I was lying on.

"You are due for your first milking and we want to knock you up so bad. That's what you want, right?" He asked, settling his hand on my thigh and sliding it up. There was no point in lying, so I just nodded. "When you are in heat, it means you'll be producing even more milk than normal. I'm addicted to it."

I had nothing to say, so I just nodded again and focused on the feeling that the pump machines were making me feel. Rounds after rounds of absolute pleasure, traveling all through my body and making my nipples hard.

I was moaning and groaning as time passed, and I realized that it was going to be difficult to imagine what my life was going to be like when I was pregnant. I didn't worry about that too much, though.

All I wanted right now was having their immense dicks inside me and shooting their come all over my walls.

Walter settled his hands on my thighs, opening me up. Otis was now standing right in front of me.

His dick was so big that even if he was grabbing it with both of his hands, it wouldn't be enough. That was just how big he was, his balls hanging very low and looking hot like lava. Heavy with his come, I couldn't wait to have another taste of it.

He took a step forward as he pried open my mouth with his hand and slid his dick into it. He didn't go all the way, realizing that even though he could be doing that, it wouldn't bring him the pleasure he was looking for.

And I felt how hot he was by having his shaft inside of me like this. Swirling my tongue around it, I started to give him a blowjob that he was going to remember for the rest of his life.

Brushing my tongue under his dickhead, I made him throw his head backward as he grabbed my head and started to move it up and down.

He still wasn't going all the way inside, which was something I was thankful for. I was happy with how things were. I was sucking him off and losing my mouth virginity for the second time.

And I was saying that because the first time counted and didn't at the same time.

Giving a bull a blowjob was different when I was a hucow. Much, much different, and also much better.

Then, I was squirming and my body was thrashing about when a wave of pleasure ran through my body. It made me arch my toes and curve my back. When I was done, I was panting and my mouth was still watering.

I was thirsty and wasn't at the same time. It was a weird feeling, but also one that I welcomed.

CHAPTER 5

Otis wasn't done with me, but now I was focusing my attention on the guy behind me. He was lining up his cock to my pussy, which was exposed and begging for him to penetrate me. I was shivering at the thought of what he was going to do once he was in there.

"Please…" I said, my voice weaker than it had ever been.

And then I heard a slap against my ass, and it was so hard that it made me arch my back. He was rough and demanding, and I needed to keep that in mind.

"You lost every chance you had to stop this, bitch," Walter's voice rumbled in the semi-darkness of the barn, and all the other hucows mooed in response.

I heard their bells jingling all over. My bell was hanging from the collar on my neck, and it was also jingling gently as I moved my body.

He dug his fingers into my skin, took a step forward, pushed his hips, and then pierced my cunt with everything he had. He wasn't being gentle like his friend was, and I was happy that he was doing things this way.

Walter's speed was intense from the get-go, his balls slapping off my ass. He was reaching a spot inside of me I never thought possible, and now that I was thinking about it, he must have popped my hymen already, and I didn't even notice it. It was a pity. It was the moment where I was no longer a virgin.

"Fuck, you're really so tight," he commented, his fingers digging in so deep that, for a moment, I thought he was going to draw out blood.

I was thankful that didn't happen, and I was even more thankful for all the kinds of sensations he was rewarding me with. I was groaning and orgasming with each of his thrusts, and I never thought that this was going to be so good.

In the meantime, the pump machines hadn't stopped working. They were still squirting out my milk and filling the gallons by one of the walls of the barn. What they were thinking they were going to do with all that milk, I didn't know, but seeing that was piquing my curiosity again.

I didn't have much time to think about that as Walter bumped his pace and held me still, his dick suddenly throbbing and shooting jet after jet of his come.

It was painting all of my walls, and it was hot and thick. I didn't expect anything different coming from him.

"Oh, fuck, that was so good," he said, his voice low like before.

And just when I thought I was going to have some time to say anything back to him, I remembered I still had Otis' dick in my mouth.

He was still ramming it in and out, and his balls were finally tensing up. He was going to come inside my mouth, and it was everything I wanted right now.

His dick exploded as he shot rope after rope of his delicious come down my throat. It was so salty and I loved it. And he had so much milk in his balls he was making me wonder when it was the last time he had sex or jerked off. I couldn't ask him that, so all I did was to keep moaning while his massive dick stuffed my stomach.

After a moment, he started to slowly pull out of my mouth. As he did that, I realized that his shaft was so slick and gluey with his come that a line of it stuck to my mouth.

It split in two only when he was well out of my mouth. And the part of the line that was still on my lips, I promptly licked it up.

Walter, having pulled out, rounded the table and stood in front of me.

"Time for us to change things up a bit, don't you think, brother?" He said, opening my mouth with his fingers and sliding his dick inside it. I didn't have another choice but to accept it, and I'd been craving it this whole time anyway.

I still had to stretch my lips quite a bit so that it could fit, but once it was in there, it was like I was in heaven. His colleague didn't waste a single second before easing his prick into my fanny and starting to pound in and out.

His pace was frenetic from the get-go, and I was loving everything about it. I was matching him thrust for thrust, and he wasn't going to stop until he was putting his heir in my belly.

My boobs already felt a little empty and the machine was exerting greater force to keep taking out more of my milk. Both of the huge, perfect cowboys then climaxed inside me.

My holes were sore, but I was still begging for them to continue. They slapped my face and ass, leaving red marks on my skin that were never going to fade away.

They both pulled out and I was left panting, alone with my thoughts. I hadn't just lost my virginity today.

They'd just finished knocking me up and soon I was going to have their heirs in my belly. And when that happened, I was pretty sure that our fucks were going to be a lot tastier.

I was in heaven.

COWBOYS' NAUGHTY AGE GAP

Fertile First Time Holiday Story

CHAPTER 1

I was bending down for a bucket I dropped when I felt a hand cupping my ass. I whirled around, meeting the eyes of one of the men that put me in this place. And 'put me here' was the right way to describe it.

I shouldn't be here, but I still was because I was doing a favor for someone important.

The man was shirtless, chewing straw in his mouth, his hands on his waist, and was eating me alive with his eyes.

I had a checkered shirt on that left my belly exposed, tight shorts that didn't help much when it came to hiding my asscheeks, and a pair of boots so that my feet weren't hurt while I strolled around his farm.

The hair on his chest seemed to draw the attention of my eyes, and I couldn't stop looking at it.

But I was forcing myself not to do that because the incisive eyes of the man who paid my salary were looking straight into my soul, and he was telling me a million things with that stare.

Sweat drops were ri, veleting down his body. His hands were big and he could cup my asscheeks and make them feel smaller than they really were, even though I was a little chubbier. His skin was a little rough and 'textured', showing the age gap between us.

He was so much taller than me that I'd have to get on my toes to kiss him, not that I was thinking about doing something so antiquated with him. I was thinking about the huge shaft that he probably had.

He wasn't the kind of man that liked to keep it hidden from the prying eyes of a woman like me. More often than not, after diving in the swimming pool on their farm, he jumped out of the water and his speedo always seemed to be clinging to his skin. I wanted to find out how thick and big he was.

It was something for another time, though.

And I also couldn't stop ogling the perfect curves of his muscles. Each seemed to have been made specifically for him. And the interesting thing about them was that he didn't work out. At all.

He spent so much time tending to his animals and running the farm he didn't have space in his schedule for that. He didn't take supplements or anything like that as well. He was a natural, and I loved that about him.

I put my hands up as I tried to excuse myself from here. It was the only way to get out of this place without feeling like I was building a case where he could kick me out without feeling any kind of remorse.

The only reason why I was working for him and living here was that I needed the money.

Someone I deeply cared about needed me to buy some expensive medicine for her, and this was the only way to do it.

But thinking that wasn't going to stop him, of course. "I'm sorry, but I need to go, and those hucows won't feed themselves."

"I know," he grumbled, shooting his hand to my arm and grabbing it. I should be fuming that he was grabbing me like this without showing any remorse, but the fact was that I was feeling the opposite of that. His hand was firm and it was gripping my arm without hurting me.

Otis knew what he was doing, the line that he was crossing, and he wasn't bothered by that one bit.

"But I'm stopping you now before you do anything stupid. I've been thinking about you and that you're a perfect candidate to become one of them. As you know, the herd isn't going to grow on its own. Not until after some time has passed anyway."

I bit my bottom lip. I wasn't going to deny that I knew what offer he was making me. Otis wanted me to turn into a hucow, and that was a lot more than I thought I was going to get coming here.

I wanted to slide my hands over his stubble and feel his chin, but I'd said to them when I came here that I had a boyfriend, and I didn't want to come out of this barn feeling like an idiot. I also wasn't going to say to them that I was a virgin, too.

They'd look at that and the first thing they would think was that I needed their big, hard cocks impaling me. I knew that they would be in the right, and I was already licking my lips in anticipation, but I didn't want to subject myself to something like that.

Not while I'd feel like an idiot who didn't know anything about life.

Otis took a step forward, putting himself right in front of me. He was so much taller than me that if I were looking straight ahead, I'd only be seeing his nipples.

And I could see that they were hard and perky. Not only that, but the bulge in his jeans was getting noticeable. It was growing and I knew what that meant.

The thought that I should be suing him for taking advantage of his employee wasn't stopping me from feeling so wet I was going to have to change my panties later.

He eased his grip on my arm when he realized that I wasn't going anywhere. Not that I could when his eyes were set on me and he was staring at me as if he was looking into my soul.

Every fiber of my being was telling me to stop this and run away from this place as soon as possible, but the biggest part in me was showing me otherwise.

It was showing me that I could take the next step and live my life to its fullest on his farm.

Growing with the other hucows, mooing with them, swallowing his come down my throat, and then having his dick shoved up my ass multiple times a day.

The thought of doing both of those things was already making me feel so wild I was making a decision I was going to regret.

CHAPTER 2

I was in a very dark place and Walter was lining up his cock to the hucow's waiting hole. The way she was lifting her ass and mooing was showing me what thoughts were going on in her mind.

Sweat drops were flowing down her body and her boobs were swinging back and forth as milk dripped out of them.

Walter had a dirty smile on his face, and he was making no attempts to hide it. I knew what the purpose of this moment was. He was doing it to convince me that making the choice he wanted me to make was the right thing for me.

And he was building a very good case for himself. His dick was thick, long, veiny, and come was oozing out of it. If I were making a different choice than the one I was making right now, I would be thrilled at the thought of getting on my knees and wrapping my lips around that thing.

Not only that, but he was also naked from top to bottom. He was so turned on that his balls were redder than they normally were. And I was saying that because I knew what they looked like when he wasn't feeling this way.

He also said to me that they were bigger because he was a bull. Him being different than a normal man meant that he made a lot more come than other men.

He settled his hands on the hucow's waist and started to ease it in. And the moment he did that, I felt like I was the hucow. I felt like he was drilling that thing inside of me and stretching my walls beyond their limits.

I felt like he was now reaching the end of my womb and was only stopping when he felt he couldn't go any further.

"Do you see what I'm doing to her?" He asked, his fingers digging into her body, and I was only wondering if she was feeling pain or not. If she was, then I would be begging him to let me swap places with her so that I was the one on the receiving end. "And do you see what her face looks like?"

I didn't have to ask him what he meant. He wanted me to feel jealous of her and it was working. My hands were becoming like balls and my nipples were hard and erect.

Her name was Judy. She was a new hucow that now lived with us, and she was happy beyond measure that she was living here now. Her life as a hucow was all about getting fucked multiple times a day, milked, and nurturing the cowboys' heirs in her huge belly.

And the other thing she told me about it being like that was that when she was in heat and pregnant, that she made a lot more milk than she normally did.

I could see that in the way that the milk was dripping out of her nipples and was wetting the hay on the ground. I was more than feeling jealous at this point. I was feeling like punching her and then killing her so that I could steal her place.

When Walter was all the way inside her, he let a moment of nothingness pass. He was only doing that because he was kinder than Otis. The latter was a lot more brutal.

He fucked all the hucows every day, and I knew that if I decided to turn into one of them, the first thing that would happen was that he would be the one taking my virginity.

A minute or so later, Walter was ramming it in and out of her, and the look of pleasure on his face was palpable. I could even hear his balls slapping on her butt, and that was making me feel so unlike my normal self I was already beginning to wonder what I was doing with my life.

I could be the one doing that. I could be the one getting it hammered in and growing his heirs in my belly. Walter was doing this without a condom on, and it couldn't be any different. When it came to sex, he always only did it without the flimsy rubber getting in the way.

I thought that he was already at his maximum speed, but then he kicked up his pace a few notches. Pain and pleasure were deforming Judy's face and she was drooling from both sides of her mouth. I wanted now, more than anything, to be getting underneath her just to have a better view of what was happening.

Judy was soon moaning and groaning, her body shaking wildly when she reached her climax. Walter stopped what he was doing and pressed his balls to her ass, making sure that not a drop of his come was going to leak out.

But that was something he couldn't do. Drops of his come were still leaking out and falling on the hay. Seeing that, it prompted me to make up my mind once and for all.

I got on my knees right away and stuck my tongue out. I was under Judy and licking up the come on the hay. Walter and Judy were both looking at me with wide eyes. Of all the things they thought I was going to do, that wasn't one of them.

And it was worth every dust that my tongue was feeling on the hay. Walter's come was delicious, savory, and salty. It was everything I thought it was going to be, and I was wondering how it took me so long to be doing this.

I should have made this choice a long time ago.

CHAPTER 3

Now that I made the best choice of my life, it was time for something else. I was lying across the back of the tractor, and Otis was putting my legs over his shoulders. He was ogling my pussy and I could tell that he was taking it in, enjoying every millisecond of this moment.

"Damn. Having fucked so many virgins like you, I knew that it was going to be something else, but I didn't think you had a cunt that looks so inviting. You're making me hard just looking at it."

I was giggling. I knew he was joking because he was already hard before he put me on the tractor. It was the first time that my legs were feeling the hardness of his muscles, and they were everything I thought they were going to be. They were so hard that he was making me wonder how he could keep himself in shape like this.

My transformation was still happening. Walter's come was still turning me into a hucow, and even though I was excited about it, the thing I was most thrilled about right now was him impaling me.

It shouldn't be feeling this good. The sun was hotter than normal and so was the back of the tractor. I should be feeling like my skin was burning, but I was feeling the opposite.

Rather, I should be saying that the only thing I could think about was him impregnating me with his potent milk. I couldn't wait until he was shooting it all inside of me, rewarding me with his heirs. I couldn't wait until I was matching all the other hucows when it came to making milk.

"Let's just get this over with," I said, moaning when he pressed one of his fingers to my pussy lips. We were out in the open and anyone could be seeing this.

Anyone could be seeing that a hunky, perfect cowboy was fucking a woman with breasts too big for her. It was even becoming difficult for me to walk around because of their weight.

Not that I was complaining about it. I was having the opposite reaction, in fact.

He brushed his fingers over my pussy lips, stopping when he was about to reach my clit. I thought that he was going to start rubbing his finger on it over and over, but then he stopped, forcing me to tilt my head down.

I squinted my eyes and looked at him like I was making him a question.

He curled up the corner of his lips. "What? Did you think that this was going to be so easy? You need to make me think you are worth it."

"But I am worth it," I groaned, throwing my head backward when I felt his finger pressing against my clit. It was my bundle of nerves and he knew how to hit the right spot every time he applied some pressure on it.

Otis was as cruel as I thought he was going to be, and he had every right to be like this.

"Then say the magical words. Say what I want you to say."

I bit my lower lip. I knew what he wanted and what he meant. For a moment, I thought that I should have a little more self-worth, but then I realized how that didn't make sense for me anymore. The only thing that mattered right now was getting another taste of his tasty come.

"Please, fuck me hard and put your heirs in my belly," I said out loud and clearly, and that widened the smile on his face. I knew he was going to have that reaction, which was why I was happy when he put his hands on my waist and started to pierce my slit with his massive cock.

I bit my lower lip harder when I realized that he was bigger than I thought. He was stretching my walls beyond all the levels

I thought possible, pushing through every barrier he found, and then I heard something pop. Or maybe I just felt it happening.

When that happened, Otis stopped. His hands were still holding my waist, and his fingers were slightly grazing my skin. I felt like everything around me was freezing up. I couldn't even hear the moo of the hucows in the barn behind me.

"How are you feeling?" He asked, and I was surprised those words came out of his mouth. I thought that he was incapable of feeling anything for someone else.

"Better than before," I responded and that earned me the reaction I was hoping I was going to get from him. Otis pulled me with force, breaking through all the other barriers, and stopping when he reached the end of my moist tunnel.

Feeling like I couldn't let him go anywhere right now for anything, I was squeezing him with my walls. We were knotted and he was only going to be leaving now after he came inside me.

A moment of nothingness ensued. Otis was inside of me to the hilt and was probably counting the seconds until he was ramming me with his impressive cock. I could feel it slightly throbbing inside of me, which was showing me how close he was to blowing his come out.

I couldn't wait until he was impregnating me with so many heirs it would be hard for me to count them all.

My hands went for my breasts and I started to play with them. I pinched my nipples and squeezed my boobs vigorously, little moans escaping my mouth when I felt him pistoning in and out of me.

Just like I knew it was going to be like with him, he was ramming his slab of meat in and out of me, and I couldn't see any pity in his eyes. My body kept grazing on the back of the tractor and even though it should be hurting me more than it was, I didn't think about stopping.

Not until this beast of a man was filling me up with his sperm.

A moment later, his dick erupted inside of me and I squealed and mooed. There was nothing like feeling that we were building something that could never be broken.

A moment later, he pulled out. I noticed that drops of his come were dripping onto the seat of the tractor, and the first thought that popped up in my mind was that it was a waste.

But now my initiation ritual was complete and the next step was to get my first milking.

I couldn't wait until they were fucking me while the machine was pumping my milk out of my boobs.

CHAPTER 4

I was suspended in the air when the pumps were latched onto my boobs. I felt the pressure they were applying the moment I heard a click. A strap was over my eyes, and it was dark and I couldn't see anything.

They said that my first milking was going to be much better when the only thing I could focus on was the process itself.

Being suspended in the air didn't mean that they couldn't touch me. In fact, I felt a hand touching one of my ass cheeks, moving in circles as he felt it for what it was.

"You are so tasty. Your body is perfect."

That was Walter who was speaking, and his voice was as manly as ever. His fingers were slightly digging into my skin, and I knew what was going on in his mind. I knew what his plan was for when he was fucking me again.

A heard someone pressing a button, and then the machine was whirring to life. It was quite loud and the noise was filling the space inside the barn.

They were both watching me while it was working, and I could feel the pumps applying moments of pressure, and those moments of pressure led to milk squirting out my boobs.

The reason why they were doing this was that they needed my milk to sell it, and also because my boobs were aching. Now that I was in heat and my body was huger than it had ever been, I was making much more milk than normal.

And that milk needed to go somewhere.

"Damn, she really makes a lot of milk. She is going to become one of our top hucows in no time," Otis said, feeling me with his hands and then sliding one of his fingers over my clit. He was then pressing it against it and making me beg to have him drive his dick inside of me.

I was pretty sure that he was thinking the same thing.

"She's going to be all mine when this is over," Walter said and I could feel a rift opening between the two of them. Even Otis started to press his finger to my bundle of nerves more tightly.

They were competitive men, after all. I knew that this meant a lot more than it met the eyes.

The pumps of the machine were still squirting out my milk, and I could already feel that it was making a difference. My breasts were feeling less heavy as time passed. I was where all the other hucows could see me, and I was pretty sure they were feeling jealous that I was getting my first milking.

Neither Walter nor Otis said anything, the machine beginning to apply more pressure to get the last drops out of my boobs.

When they were feeling so much lighter that it was like they were empty, the cowboys decided to press the button on the machine again.

It stopped working and then I felt that what was keeping me suspended in the air was now turning me around. It was making it so I was upside down and my cunt was where they needed it to be.

One of the cowboys leaned in, putting his nose next to it. He took a long, audible sniff at it that sent shivers down my spine. I couldn't wait until he was doing that many more times when we were alone in his room. Or together with Walter. Choosing a favorite stud was so difficult.

"She's ready," he said, lowering me now until my slit was level with his dick. The strap over my eyes was still hiding pretty much everything I should be seeing, but I could tell that he was stroking his dick gently. He was going to ram that thing inside me, and there was nothing about that I could do.

"I know," Walter growled, pulling me until he was drilling into me with his shaft. It was long and thick as always, but now that I'd already lost my virginity, he was pushing it in all the way without showing an ounce of remorse on his face – not that I could see it now or anything like that, anyway. It was that, after living for so long with them, I knew everything that they did and how they acted in sexy moments like this one.

He started to ram it inside of me, his balls slapping off my buttcheeks. Him being where he was and doing what he was doing didn't mean that Otis needed to be only watching everything.

He walked until he was standing right behind me and then seized my thighs until he was inserting his long shaft up my asshole.

He broke through every barrier and now that he was doing this with me for the first time, I felt like I was losing my virginity again. Losing my butthole's virginity, to be more precise.

But that really was just a drop in the ocean of things that were going on with me right now.

A moment later, they were both coming inside of me. They swapped places and roles, extending our fuck until it felt like it had already been hours since it started. Both of my holes were aching, but that still left one other hole that they hadn't explored yet.

My mouth.

CHAPTER 5

They took me off the machine and then out of the barn. We had a swimming pool on the farm. They put me inside the water, and I was happy that it wasn't too deep. My feet could touch the floor and I could support myself in the water without feeling like I was going to fall over because of the water moving.

We decided to do something different this time. They were going to be less rough with me here.

They were both sitting on the edge of the swimming pool, and they were stroking their dicks as they realized this was the last thing we were going to be doing for today.

Now that I was seeing their shafts so up close, it was difficult not to notice all the details that I missed before. Before this, I had to kind of pretend I wasn't seeing what I was now seeing.

Their dicks were so lust-inducing, all the veins that I hadn't noticed before, how visible the little slits were, and how low their balls hung.

I was going to give them a blowjob, one at a time, and it was going to be a difficult decision to make who I should please first. Walter was a little longer, but Otis was somewhat thicker and his balls were slightly heavier, too.

I was taking in this spectacular view that I was having, and the only thought swirling around in my mind was how I was going to approach this. Without giving it another thought, I chose the guy on the left and approached his balls, opening my lips.

It was Otis, and I couldn't believe that I was going to give him a blowjob. Not long before now, he was ramming his thick tool in and out of my pussy, and it had been a wonderful experience. He'd hurt me so much and had made me feel so much pain at the same time…

I couldn't wait until we were doing it again.

I wrapped my lips around his manhood, grabbed his balls, and started to do my thing. I didn't have much experience doing this and I was hoping that they were all going to forgive me for that.

Moving my fingers against his balls and bobbing up and down on him, I was making sure that I was hitting all the sweet spots I thought he had.

"Yeah, that's it. Like that, ohhhh…" The man mumbled, which only served to propel me to keep this up. I loved how wet his meat was, how hot it seemed to pulse in my mouth, and all the veins pumping his blood continuously. Nothing was better than this.

He was putting his hand on my head now and was pushing it down and pulling it up. He was grabbing my hair, but not too tightly. I didn't feel any pain, just that he was making me follow his desired rhythm.

His hands were moving over my body, finding my breasts, cupping them, and then he even reached over to plant a hickey on my neck. I squirmed and let it happen. I mean, was there even anything I could do against it? I didn't think so.

Kicking up my sucking-him-off pace a couple of notches, Otis' dick was soon throbbing in my mouth and it took me a lot of effort not to let it slip out. He was then shooting his come inside it, and it was salty, tasty, and a little tacky, too.

I moved my head up, kissed the tip of his cock for good luck, cleaned up the entirety of the shaft, and then moved over to the other cowboy. He was sporting a straw hat on his head and was smoking a cigarette.

He didn't toss it aside when he saw me slowly walking in the water. It was already difficult walking outside thanks to the weight of my boobs, and thus I was finding it surprising that I was actually managing to do this.

"You better make this last, Lena," he growled and I felt a shiver of fear running down my spine. I wasn't going to disappoint him. That was something I was promising myself.

And so, doing that, I started things by grabbing his balls and playing with them for a little while. I heard the sound of water splashing and moving viciously, like something heavy had been dropped in it, and I realized that it was Otis. After the amazing blowjob he got, now he wanted to swim a little and think about something else.

Or think about fucking another hucow. Either worked for him.

I soon wrapped my lips around the monster cock of the man in front of me and started my routine of moving my head up and down on it. He was so long that he kept hitting the back of my throat.

He kept making me feel like gagging and coughing, but I held those things back. I just wanted to find out what his taste was like, and I was going to make that happen soon enough. I was sure of it.

His balls were even hotter now in my hands, and they were hanging so low and were so heavy that I was having a bit of a hard time playing with them. Moving them up and down on my fingers, and then between them, alongside the way I was swirling my tongue around his dickhead, it took him very little time to be pumping out his load.

The man was creaming inside my mouth and I was working hard to swallow everything. But I heard some drops falling onto the floor around the swimming pool, which was disappointing and was like arrows piercing my heart.

He moaned and then I was pushing myself up out of the swimming pool, sticking my tongue out with just one purpose in mind - I wasn't going to let his drops go to waste, and so I was already licking them off the floor even though it was a little dirty.

Walter dove into the water and was now swimming with his colleague. They were smiling from ear to ear and I felt like I belonged in a family.

I wouldn't change this life for anything.

COWBOYS' CHRISTMAS AGE GAP

Fertile First Time Holiday Story

CHAPTER 1

I was seated on the couch and I couldn't stop moving my hands. The cowboy was seated on the other couch, and he was looking at me with mischievous eyes. It was snowing outside and it was quite cold in the room, but I was still finding it pretty hot.

As time went by, I started to think that coming here was a mistake, especially for Christmas. I just thought that I was going to come here to make some extra money, but I could already see that I wasn't on a normal farm.

Seated beside me was a friend of mine. Her name was Phyllis and she was of German descent, just like me. Looking at her, I could see that she was feeling just as nervous as I was. She was sweating a little and I could see she wanted to get out of here as soon as possible.

But that was something we couldn't do. We came here, the farm was too far from everything, and we didn't have money anymore for a trip back home.

His bulge was growing big in his pants, and the way he was moving his hand over it was making me think that he was sexually thinking about me. Moving my fingers through my hair, I was trying to smile and pretend that I wasn't feeling as nervous as I was.

The cowboy was saying something about tending to his barn, but the words were coming through one ear and going out through the other.

He wore heavier clothes to fight against the cold, and I could tell that it was working for him. He wasn't looking at all cold and was pretty comfortable where he was seated. And it wasn't just that one cowboy that was here with us, too.

His friend was also with us and he was just as big as his work colleague. He was behind the other couch and both of his hands were in his pockets. I could see how big they were and how veiny they appeared to be. I wondered what it would feel like to have those hands roaming over my body… He looked like the kind of man that could find every spot and nerve in my body.

"So, as I was saying, you're going to have to feed the hucows…" He said and even though the word 'hucows' was a bit odd to me, I didn't think much of it. It was just like it was a couple of seconds ago.

His words were going over my head and his muscles – his perfect body – was making it very difficult for me to think about what was happening here. All I could think about was that he was making me wonder what he was like when naked.

After a moment, his friend said, "Hey, Brandy, are you even listening to what we are saying?" He asked and I gulped. It was one thing pretending that everything was fine and another to know that he knew something was wrong with me.

He took his hands out of his pockets and started to go around the couch. Now that he was some feet closer to me, he looked even bigger than before. I wasn't kidding when I said he made me feel small even though I was a little chubby.

He raised one of his eyebrows and asked, "Is everything alright?"

I didn't even dare to stand up even though I should be doing that and asserting that I wasn't the desperate farmhand he was thinking I was. It was just that his pants were pretty tight around his crotch, highlighting his bulge. And just like I was thinking was happening with his friend, it was growing and I couldn't help but wonder if he was thinking about fucking me too.

I could just imagine what he would do if he was allowed to have his way with me.

Not thinking too much about that, I stood up and responded, "Y-yeah, everything's fine. I was just thinking that…"

"You were thinking what?" He asked, putting his hand on my shoulder and crossing a line I thought he wasn't going to.

After a moment of silence, he breathed in my smell and said, "You smell really nice. Like a bouquet. Like something I'd find in a marriage, or a very peculiar Christmas party…"

Behind him, I could see a Christmas tree and the little lights blinking in the branches. It was pretty and it was making me want to go to it, but my mind was focused on something else right now.

The man standing in front of me was so warm that he was making me sweat, even though the temperatures were still dropping outside.

Walter moved his hand up and I could feel how rough his palm was. He wasn't ashamed of it and that he was kind of taking advantage of someone much younger than him. In fact, he was smiling.

When I thought he was going to kiss me, he did the opposite. His hand went for his belt and started to undo it. A moment later, it was falling to the floor with a soft thud.

My eyes went down and my mouth flew open. I was looking at his pant-less legs and wondering how he could be so big. I wasn't thinking that what he was doing was wrong, but that it was exactly what I was waiting for.

My pussy was wet and my panties were getting soaked through. My legs were rubbing against each other and the only thing I was thinking about was what he was planning on doing with me right now.

He moved his hand up until it was behind my shoulder. Widening his dirty smile, he said, "Come with me. There's something I want to do with you."

I looked behind my shoulder and saw that my friend was also

coming with me. She was with the other cowboy, and I just realized that, while we were talking, so were they. She was coming along because she was willing to do what he wanted as well.

I had no idea what they had in store for us, but I knew that it was going to be painful and pleasing at the same time.

CHAPTER 2

I had no idea what I was doing when he was pushing up his cock against my mouth. It was the biggest and thickest thing I had seen in my life. His pre-come was coming out of the slit.

The man placed his hand on the back of my head and made me lower my head. I couldn't help but feel a little amount of pain when I realized that his shaft was so big he was stretching my lips.

I supposed I couldn't also tell him that this was the first time I was having sex with someone. I mean, what would a big, powerful cowboy like him think of that? He would laugh at me and kick me out of here.

"Another virgin… Nice…" He growled, shoving my head down with force and making me feel like pushing myself off of him. But I didn't need to do that because I was exactly where I needed to be, with his thick and impressive shaft filling my mouth.

Out of instinct, my hand went for his balls and I started to caress them. This being my first time, I didn't realize that I was touching balls much bigger than they were supposed to be.

A normal man didn't have nuts of these dimensions. And not only that, but they also felt pretty heavy. I couldn't wait until he was blowing his load in my mouth and I was tasting how salty it was.

I was pretty sure he was extremely potent and I couldn't wait until he was gracing my mouth with his load.

"Ready for this?" Walter asked, only to start shoving my head up and down without waiting for my answer. All I could feel was the hot friction of his dick going up and down repeatedly, and I didn't know how much longer I was going to resist all the pain he was inflicting on me.

Right by my side was Phyllis, who was in the same position that I was. Otis was ramming his dick in and out of her mouth.

They both said that we needed to swallow their sperm to 'become' something 'more special' to them, and I couldn't wait to find out if they were joking about that or not.

As time went by while my hands kept playing with his balls, they revealed we were going to become their next 'hucows.' And then, they explained everything…

One of the so-called hucows was already getting into the room, licking Walter's legs. She moved up and started to tongue his balls, making him close his eyes while I saw what was about to happen.

He was going to unload his cream inside my mouth much faster than I thought it was going to happen, and that was the biggest disappointment of the night for me.

I thought I was going to make this last a lot longer.

And, it was happening, and I could feel his balls pulsing. It wasn't too long then until he was squirting his come inside my mouth, making me vibrate with him. It was like my body was becoming one with him and all I could think about was how tasty his cream was. It was salty, very heavy, and there was a lot of it.

The longer it went on, the harder I found it to keep swallowing everything he was unloading in my mouth. Looking to the side, I could see that my friend Phyllis was also going through something similar, but that she was dealing with it much worse than I was.

Her cheeks were red like beet and I could see she was huffing. She was having difficulty breathing and I could feel her pain.

But there was no way I could help her, so I focused on swallowing everything that this guy was rewarding me with. A moment later, he was smiling as he kept stuffing my mouth with his sperm.

And this whole time, the only thing I could think about was that I was finally going to turn into a hucow.

They had let me see what they were like when I was in the barn. I looked at them and the first thought that came into my mind was that it was exactly what I wanted. I wanted to be naked like them, to have breasts as big as theirs, and to think about sex all day long.

Walter pulled out at about the same time his friend did. I looked at his shaft and wasn't surprised when I found out that it was so messy it needed a good, thorough clean.

And so, with no other thought in mind, the next thing I did was to put my tongue out and start licking it from base to top. Feeling his shaft rubbing and grazing against my tongue was even hotter than what it was like before, and it turned me on so hard I came again. I had come several times while they were fucking us.

"Tomorrow is going to be a very special day for you. I won't take you to the barn because it's not appropriate. It's too cold for someone like you. But when you're ready, I will take you there and I will put my heirs in your belly."

Otis caressed Phyllis' chin before walking out, and the look on her face was telling me everything I needed to know. She never thought that our blowjob was going to be so hard and rewarding at the same time.

And tomorrow, after our transformation was complete, we were going to have even more of that.

CHAPTER 3

I never thought that my day was going to be like this. I was in the kitchen and Otis was right behind me. He was already inside of me. Rolling his hips, he was fucking me beyond anything I thought it was going to be like.

The man was ruthless, blasting his balls against my ass. Now that I was finally a hucow, milk kept shooting out of my teats as I followed his pace.

Every time he pounded into my butt, drops of my milk shot out in different directions. It was difficult for me to keep up with him, and the way he was fucking me was already making me beg for air.

But it wasn't like he was letting me breathe properly, either. He had his hand on my mouth, covering it as he dug his fingers into my skin.

I should be angry he was doing this with me, but I was actually feeling the opposite. My pussy was burning hot, and never before had it felt so tight. He was taking my virginity with my consent and was making me feel like a new woman.

The harder he was ramming it in, the more I was feeling like I made the best decision of my life when I decided to come here.

Outside, a snowstorm was raging and making a tree's branches sway violently. Moments later, my vision blurred when the man started to come inside me.

On the table right in front of me, my friend was also getting her fill. Walter was pounding in and out of her cunt and the slapping noises they were making made me feel even more aroused than normal.

It was just the four of us in the farmhouse and it was awesome.

"Fuck, you're so tight," Otis said before shooting out his come in my pussy. I squeezed it on him as I thought that I would only let him go after he finished coming inside of me.

Moments later, he was pressing his balls against my womb and I knew that could only mean one thing. He was just about done with me, which meant that it wasn't going to be much longer now until our first milking. I was already salivating at the thought of getting milked by these Masters.

"Yes, I know I am," I squealed, feeling like I was so fortunate that I had these two cowboys destroying everything that once made me the person I'd been.

Phyllis wasn't faring much better. She kept closing her eyes, and it almost looked like she was going to pass out. She was hanging by a thread while her cowboy kept destroying every last vestige of her virginity. Even from afar, I could see that her cunt was redder than normal and that this was probably her fifth time climaxing.

A moment later, she was squirming and thrashing her body about under his dominance. He was holding onto her tightly and his fingers were pressing so hard into her skin it was like he was hurting her.

But even though she was feeling a lot of pain, she would never forgive me if I thought that way about what was happening.

The man pulled out of her, and I could see how her womb kept contracting and expanding, looking for him. She knew it was going to be tough to be without his shaft inside of her, but there wasn't much she could do about it.

A moment later, the cowboy's rough hands slid up and down her body, making sure that she always knew she was his for the rest of her life.

Otis pulled out of me, flipped me around, and started to maul on my boobs. His tongue was relentless, swirling around them, pressing against my teats, and then going up and down between them.

Each time he tasted me with his tongue, I felt more connected to him. And then his finger started to rub over my clit and draw circles on it. It was the perfect moment to solidify and commemorate that I was a hucow now.

When Otis wasn't inside of me anymore, I felt like my world was going to disappear. But a moment later, he was moving his hands up and down my body, stopping his fingers when they were ravaging my cunt.

Rubbing his fingers on it again, he made me feel like I was going to come several times in a row, and that was exactly what happened. My body pulsed, vibrated, and nothing was better than knowing that this sweaty cowboy was obsessed with me.

Phyllis turned her head to look at me when she fell to the floor. Her chest going up and down, I knew she was already thinking about what her next time with them was going to be like. And it was a no-brainer to me when I thought that I needed to taste her, too.

Moving slowly toward her, I didn't stop when I started to put my tongue out and rub her gaping slit. She squealed and tilted her head backward, inviting me deeper inside of her.

My head was between her legs and I could smell her scent. My tongue moving up and down and left and right, I was feeling even more connected to her.

Milk was coming out of her nipples in drops and pooling on the floor around us. And then I noticed that the cowboys were going to the living room and that our next stop was going to be there. I licked and fingered my friend's hurt pussy lips before standing up. Holding my hand out, she grabbed it and I helped her up.

We were still light enough to walk around on our two feet, but we knew that soon it was going to be different.

CHAPTER 4

This was going to be a different kind of milking than I thought it was going to be. I was still in the farmhouse, noticing that the sun was shining brightly outside. Even though it was bright, it was still not warm enough for us to go there.

We were still a little cold, and now that we didn't have logs to burn in the fireplace anymore, we were even more dependent on our bodily heats to keep ourselves warm.

The device that was holding me was a little strange. It was kind of like the part where a person was put in a guillotine, except that my boobs were connected through holes that were pressing around it. I couldn't move my body without feeling like they were going to tear my skin. Thankfully, I didn't have to move at all.

Phyllis was by my side and the question popping up in her mind was obvious. *What is going to happen now?* I could almost hear her mind saying that.

Tubes were attached to our boobs and while the machine worked, the cowboys were going to fuck us. I was already licking my lips at the thought.

"Ready for this?" I asked my friend and I could tell she was ready. She was more than that. She was begging for that to happen.

She nodded when the machine started to whir. We felt our boobs being pressed on, and then milk was coming out in hot jets.

They were filled with little bubbles and looked very white, show-ing their good quality.

The mere feeling of having those things applying pressure on our boobs was already making me lose my mind.

My vision started to darken when I felt a wave of orgasm com-ing. And then, when a pair of hands settled on my ass and started to squeeze it, I couldn't take it anymore.

I came, hard and it went on a lot longer than normal, my body in pain when the wood of the device keeping us in place started to tear my skin. Some blood came out, but not a lot of it, and the ma-chine kept doing its thing. My boobs were aching before our first milking started, and now it was like I never felt that in the first place.

A few moments later, we didn't have any more milk in our boobs anymore. Our first milking was quite taxing on us, and those cowboys knew that. They were seated on a couch and were stroking their dicks while they looked at us like they were think-ing about eating us alive.

And I was pretty sure that was going to happen. And... wait. Now that I was thinking about it, why was it that I had felt hands touching my rump before? Urgh, nothing of this made any sense.

The only thing that made sense was the fact that those hot cowboys were too hungry for us and that they were already mak-ing plans to fuck us as soon as we didn't have any more milk in our boobs.

A couple of minutes later, that was exactly what happened. Otis pressed a button and the machine moved away from us. It was compartmentalized, and I could hear something mechanic moving behind the walls and under the floor.

It was quite interesting, but I didn't think much of it. The only thing that mattered right now was that those hairy cowboys were finally standing up.

Walking toward us, Otis filled my mouth with his throbbing cock and fucked it until he was shooting his come inside of it. It was thick and creamy, just like before.

We couldn't go through the whole Hucow transformation process again and even though knowing that hurt me a little, I was satisfied enough just feeling his slow milk moving on my tongue and in my throat.

"Fuck. Nothing like having two recently ex-virgins to spice things up," Walter growled, yanking me to him and then buying his dick inside my waiting cunt.

It wasn't too long then until he was pumping me full with his load. I could only wonder how a man like him could make so much sperm in so little time like it was nothing. And he always finished inside me so often I wondered how many heirs he was going to end up slotting inside my belly.

I was huffing when they were all finished with me. Looking from side to side after falling on the floor, I wondered if this was it. They already milked us once.

They already fucked us until our wombs were in pain. That should be everything they wanted to do with us, right? But that wasn't it. They wanted more. Otis and Walter were standing around us as they kept stroking their massive dicks.

They were going to paint us with their sperm, and there was nothing about it we could do

And why would there be when this was everything we were looking for since coming here? We were their always-willing dolls and we were always going to be like that.

A moment later, I could feel those hot jets hitting every part of our body. If before the room was already smelling of sex and come, now it was even more so.

We weren't just going to be things carrying their heirs inside our bellies. We were much more than that, and thinking that brought a smile to my face.

"That's it for today," Otis said and he started to his bedroom. Cracking open a beer, I knew that we were still not done. They still wanted to do us even after we gave birth to their heirs.

And they also wanted to fuck us while we were pregnant and fill our holes with their come minutes before we went into labor. They wanted their heirs to always remember that they were born under their cum.

And that... Thinking that we were going to make that happen was already asking me mad.

CHAPTER 5

My belly was bigger than it had ever been, and now everything was so settled that I knew what was going to happen. I knew everything that was going to take place in the barn. It was still cold, especially inside there, but it was okay.

I was with the other hucows. Their bodily heats were making it so we could spend a couple of hours in here.

"Are you ready for the final act?" He asked, brushing a finger over my clit. Then, his finger stopped where my belly was. I was pregnant and I didn't know whose heir it was.

All I knew was that he was going to fuck me minutes before the scheduled pregnancy. I knew that we were soon going into labor. That was how it happened for hucows like us.

"More than ready," I cooed, roaming my hands over his body and feeling his perfect muscles. They were hard and just like I thought they were going to be.

His friend was right beside me, moving so that he was mauling on my tits again. They were aching. I had too much milk inside of them, and this was his way of doing something about that.

He turned me around so that I was on my knees on the floor. I was trying to support my weight using my hands and arms, but it was difficult. Flinching, I opened my mouth so that his friend was slotting his dick inside of it.

Walter was doing that and the smile on his face was showing that he was more than pleased with what was happening. As for me, I was just happy I was making them feel proud of themselves.

He put his hand behind my head and started to move it up and down like he owned it. And he did, I reminded myself. I always had to do that so that he didn't have to punish me.

But it wasn't like thinking that was preventing it from happening. Otis was already striking my butt with his heavy hand, slapping sounds filling the room.

My body was sweating more than it normally did, and my belly was making it feel even huger than it really was. A moment later, Otis was slotting his dick inside my body and he went so deep I thought he was going to pierce the last barrier. But that didn't happen, and he just stayed there, almost like he wanted me to get used to his size.

That was difficult to do, so I didn't think too much about it. What I thought was that I was living the best moment of my life because of these huge cowboys.

A moment later, they were both pounding in and out of me like I was more than their hucow. Maybe they were thinking about making me their most favorite hucow, but I didn't think that was possible.

Milk was leaking out of my nipples with each of their thrusts. I was feeling a lot of pain and some guilt that I was doing this without my friend. She was in the farmhouse, waiting for her turn.

She wouldn't like to know they were eating me first, so we were doing this behind her back.

A moment later, they both moaned loudly as they came inside of me. Feeling their hot come inside my womb and mouth was making me go so wild that I was trying to squeal and scream at the same time.

I had no idea how I was reacting anymore and all I knew was that I wanted to make this last as long as possible.

Otis slowly pulled out of me and, as he did that, the first thought that popped up in my mind was that I wanted him back inside of me right away.

My hole kept clenching and unclenching to make that happen, but the mischievous smile on his face was telling me he wasn't even thinking about doing that.

My hands were shaking, as were my arms. Looking up, I realized that, in the end, I was nothing to them. Their come was dripping out as I found out that it was difficult to keep all of it inside of me. I tried to swallow everything, but there were still some drops leaking out through the sides of my mouth.

And then, I felt like something weird was happening with my body. I had no idea if it was the fact that I was going into labor soon, but I didn't think much about it. All I knew was that my belly was a little in pain and that I wanted those guys back inside of me right away.

"Please…" I pleaded, but it wasn't like they were hearing me. My eyes stopped at the butt of the huge cowboy who was now leaving the barn. I could see him walking in the snow and I wanted to be right with him. I wanted him to put a collar around my neck and take me around with a leash.

But now that the other hucows were surrounding and licking me, I knew that it wasn't going to happen. I was relegated to being just another hucow in here and that was how it was going to be for the rest of my existence.

My days were going to be filled with milking, sex, blowjobs, and pretty much everything I craved. I knew that my friend was going to break up with me because we did that behind her back, but it was okay.

I wanted her to feel that way about me because of that one time she tried to steal the person who I thought was going to become my boyfriend.

In the end, I had a huge smile on my face. My life as a hucow was going to be complete.

The End

If you want more collections like this one, check these out:

Creaming the Bimbo: A Fertile Hucow MEGA Collection

Milked by Cowboys: A Hucow Milking MEGA Bundle

And leave a review if you liked this book. It helps me so much! Thank you.

SNEAK PEEK: MILKED BY ROCKSTARS

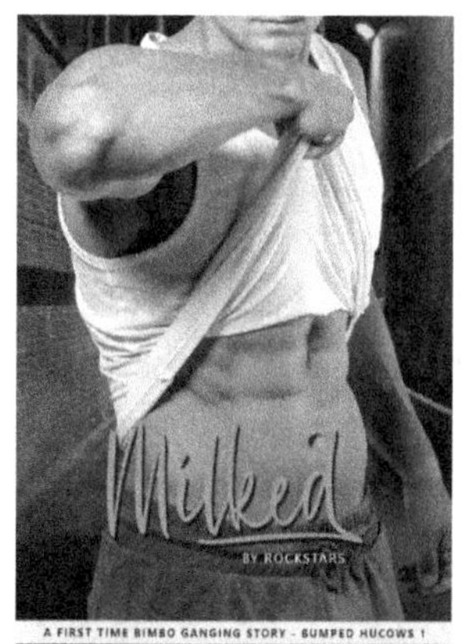

A First Time Bimbo Ganging Story

I was beyond myself. I was finally in the show that I wanted to see the most, and it was the best thing in the world. I wasn't alone, even though right now I was so. In the middle of the crowd, I didn't have anyone around me I knew. I was just another with all the other people around me.

I was dancing and shaking my arms and legs, trying to follow the pace of the song. It was unlike anything I'd heard in my life, even though I had listened to it many times before. They were my most favorite rockstars, and they were such an important part of my growing up.

The environment in the place was quite heavy, the music too loud and the people shouting and chatting around me. Blinking lights almost blinded me, and I'd still choose to be here nine times out of ten. Beads of sweat were pooling on my forehead and in my armpits, reminding me that I had already been dancing for hours. And I could still go on for a couple more hours.

It took me almost all of my money, but I was finally here in Orlando. I didn't really care about the city much. As a college student who liked those rockstars so much, all I cared about right now was to continue enjoying the heat of the moment.

Out of nowhere, a thought crossed my mind. I stopped dancing all of a sudden. It was an intrusive thought I didn't want to think about. I knew that there were problems in my life I needed to fix, but that one didn't pertain to this moment at all.

Someone bumped their shoulder against me, making me groan. It hurt me more than I thought it was going to and it was such a lack of respect I couldn't believe it. And just when I turned my head to find out who had done that, they disappeared into the crowd.

I shook my head and decided not to give that much thought. Instead of thinking about anything else, I decided to focus on the three rock stars on the platform where they were standing. They were singing like they were gods and were dancing like the wind.

I wanted to be with them, even though I knew that wasn't possible. The reason was that I was too skinny, looked too immature, and had acne on my face. If they knew about me, they would laugh at me. I was so certain about that that I couldn't even bring myself to move closer to them. Instead, I decided to keep my distance.

It was so loud I couldn't even hear my friends, even though they were calling out to me. I knew they were doing that because I saw one of them lifting his hand and shaking it over the crowd. They were probably going out to do something else. As for me, I just wanted to keep dancing.

As if by magic, one of the rockstars ripped his shirt off, showing me the perfection of his muscles. Everyone in the crowd went 'ohhhh' before resuming their frenetic dancing, bumping against each other over and over.

I'd seen many men naked in movies and there were plenty of his photos online showing him nude, but seeing the curves of his muscles and their perfection in person was still something else. And it only helped things that the lighting seemed to have been chosen to make the shadows of his muscles look more contrasting.

I felt like I was running out of air. Everyone went crazy around me, and I couldn't help but dance even more frenetically. With the main rockstar without his shirt on, he looked even more gorgeous than before. I imagined myself opening my legs for him, allowing him to come into me without difficulty.

It was such a pity that was never going to happen...

Go to the next page for even more hucow stories.

BOOKS BY THIS AUTHOR

SERIES - HUCOW FOR BLUE COLLARS

1. Milked by Plumbers: A Bimbo Ganging Story

2. Milked by Firefighters: A Bimbo Ganging Story

3. Milked by Policemen: A Bimbo Ganging Story

4. Milked by Electricians: A Bimbo Ganging Story

5. Milked by Miners: A Bimbo Ganging Story

SERIES - FERTILE ONLY

1. Bumping the Teacher: A Hucow Mafia First Time Story

2. Bumping the Midwife: A Hucow Mafia First Time Story

3. Bumping the Farmhand: A Hucow Mafia First Time Story

4. Bumping the Sinner: A Hucow Mafia First Time Story

SERIES - HUCOW FOR WHITE COLLARS

1. Milked by Lawyers: A First Time Bimbo Ménage Story

2. Milked by Doctors: A First Time Bimbo Ménage Story

3. Milked by Engineers: A First Time Bimbo Ménage Story

4. Milked by Directors: A First Time Bimbo Ménage Story

5. Milked by Managers: A First Time Bimbo Ménage Story

And you can also get these fertile hucow mega bundles:

1. Milked for Christmas: 15 First Time Hucow Stories

2. Fertile Leakers: 10 Milking Stories

3. Milked, Shared and Used: 16 Stories of Milking Ladies

ABOUT THE AUTHOR

Leandra Camilli's obsession? Writing dirty, steamy stories that make her readers drool. She loves her Alpha males, hucows, sissies, and futas. If you're looking for those kinds of books, look no further.

With a cup of coffee on her table and warm socks on, she writes almost every day. Leandra Camilli has featured in several top 100 categories in the store, and she publishes weekly.

www.ingramcontent.com/pod-product-compliance
Lightning Source LLC
Chambersburg PA
CBHW052127150726
48002CB00006B/2517